The Diary of Maggie, A Madison Mouse

Peyton Cockrill Lewis

ISBN-10: 145642145X
EAN-13: 9781456421458
LCCN: 2010918092

The Diary of Maggie, A Madison Mouse

The Seamstress At Work

CHAPTER ONE

A Proper Introduction

Orange County Virginia
Montpelier Plantation
June 1824

Dear Diary,

Today I take pen in paw to create something new in history . . . the very first mouse journal. I have confidence in my ability to write because I have long studied the master of this house, none other than James Madison, the nation's fourth president and Father of the United States Constitution.

I am too young to have sat at Mr. Madison's feet when he developed that famous document here at Montpelier, but I have witnessed his daily writing since he retired from the presidency. I have even, upon occasion, taken the liberty to improve upon his letters—to add a missing comma or to put more ink on a shaky punctuation mark. You see, Mr. Madison is afflicted with rheumatism and on some days he writes with a faint hand, given the stiffness in his joints.

But let me introduce myself, Dear Diary. I am Margaret Smith-Mouse, Maggie to my friends. I am a member of that distinguished society, **The First Families of Virginia Mice (FFVM)**. Oh, humans make much of the First Families of Virginia: the Washingtons, the Jeffersons, and the Lees. But what, Dear Diary, has been written of the FFVM?

Our family is revered in stories that go back to our arrival as part of the British party that landed on the shores of Jamestown, Virginia, in 1607. Although it's true that mice already lived in the fields and forests of the New World, we were among the first English-speaking mice to make our home here.

More recently, when this house, Montpelier, was completed, my great-great-great-great grandmother . . . oh, I don't know exactly how many greats . . . but legend has it that she was great indeed for she had the courage to cling underneath a wooden chair that was carried into the new mansion by none other than fourteen-year-old James Madison himself.

I am a middle mouse, number fifty in a total of one hundred children. As you can well imagine, I have spent my life trying to stand out from my brothers and sisters. The fact that I am the only one of the hundred who has bothered to learn to read and write would surely set me in the front ranks, but I'm afraid my mother didn't set much store in literacy.

I am also the only one in the family who has bothered to move away from the basement, choosing a place in the wall of the upstairs bedroom that provides the best view of the Blue Ridge Mountains of any room in the Madisons' house. Although I have never seen the ocean, I have heard that those blue mountains look like splendid waves crashing on a distant shore.

But before I write another word about myself, I must tell you more about my dear Dolley Payne Todd Madison. She is quite the ideal woman in thought, word, and deed. But Diary, she is also the ideal in dress. Her fashions are the latest from France, and her elegant turbans are admired far and wide. Is it any wonder that, in the deepest respect for Mrs. Madison, I have taken to dressing just the way she does?

I have very sharp teeth, you see, and I am able to remove small samples of Mrs. Madison's fabrics from the underside of her hems. It doesn't take much material to make a mouse dress, after all, and I am so professional that I have only once heard Mrs. Madison mention that she had a piece of cloth missing from her skirt. She merely reckoned that she had torn it on some bramble or other.

I must close now, Dear Diary, because today is officially the beginning of summer. That means it is time for me to store away my beautiful winter frocks. When I do that, I always like to add a sprig of lavender from the garden to keep them fresh through the hot months. As a rule, I avoid going out in the midday sun for fear its rays will bleach my chestnut brown fur, but I need to go now. Later in the afternoon, Mrs. Madison is hosting one of her famous barbecues. I must allow time to get ready. I will write again as soon as possible.

A Catastrophe

CHAPTER TWO

The Perilous Path

Maggie was dressed in her new yellow calico dress as she strolled down the garden path, taking time to enjoy the smell of flowers, as well as the scent of rosemary, basil, and thyme. The sky was a bright blue, dotted with white clouds that reminded her of puffy dandelion heads gone to seed. Ah, what a wonderful world it is, she thought, and what a fortunate mouse I am.

She had enough time before the party began to take pleasure in the garden's bounty, so she decided to search for a few delicacies for lunch: maybe the tip of an asparagus spear . . . or a nip of strawberry . . . or a bite of fresh spinach leaf to munch on. The possibilities were endless, and she couldn't imagine why she didn't go outside more often.

Moving along with great satisfaction, she was surprised to find herself walking beneath a dark shadow. A few drops of moisture fell on her head.

How could it be raining on such a sunny day? When she looked up toward the sky, however, she discovered something far, far more horrifying than any raincloud. Standing above her, showing its enormous teeth, drooling its slimy saliva on her, was a huge, bushy, snarling orange cat. And the jaws of the cat were just about to seize none other than Maggie Mouse. Instead of eating lunch, she was going to BE lunch.

Maggie ran as fast as she could, darting in a zigzag pattern down the garden path, but she couldn't run faster than the cat. The animal lunged just as Maggie jumped to the right. The cat's teeth bit into her yellow skirt and lifted Maggie high in the air. The cat shook Maggie back and forth and up and down until the garden became a whirling mass of green before her eyes. The frustrated cat shook Maggie even harder, and the little mouse became dizzier and dizzier. She could feel the cat's hot breath blowing on the fur of her neck.

Just as Maggie thought the end of her life had come, however, she heard a ripping sound and found herself flying through the air until she land-ed face down in the dirt and slid under the pro-tection of a large rhubarb leaf. Although she was breathing heavily, she managed to lie very still, her fear keeping her silent. Through the leaves she could see the cat frantically running through the garden, its yellow eyes blazing, her dress still in its mouth. Finally it spit out the fabric with a disgusted look and stalked away.

Maggie decided that, although she loved many of her clothes, she would love the yellow calico best of all. It was certainly the only garment that had ever saved her life. Finding a sprig of lavender would have to wait until another day.

Dazzled by Beauty

CHAPTER THREE

The Fateful Barbecue

Oh, Dear Diary,

Never, never in my life have I been so frightened! Out of my wits, I tell you. I was almost devoured by a cat! I have seen cats before, skulking around the barns, and I have heard family stories about treacherous encounters with cats, but I have never before been attacked by one myself. I can assure you, I will do everything possible to avoid such an experience again.

But I must pull myself together and put this incident behind me. Any minute I am expecting a visit from my favorite niece, Anna Mouse. I don't want her to see me in such a state. Anna views me as a role model, and I don't want her to witness me as a cowering wretch.

She is the daughter of my sister Susan, who I am ashamed to say has fallen on low ways. Susan married a basement mouse, the deplorable Brutus, who has completely abandoned his job of caring for his family and thinks of nothing but hiding in the wine cellar, hoping to find a few spilled drops of alcohol or broken bottles that still harbor small amounts of liquor. Susan had the misfortune of meeting Brutus at just such a barbecue as the one we are celebrating today. I will be vigilant to see that the same thing does not happen to my dear little Anna.

* * * *

Maggie closed the cover of her diary with a dramatic flourish and shook her shoulders, trying to relax. She stored the journal under her table and crossed the floor to observe herself in the looking glass.

She was proud of her mirror, for Maggie was a proud mouse in almost every way. She had discovered the shard of mirror in Dolley's bedroom. In the blackest of night, she had installed it in her cozy home. She positioned the glass just at the entrance to her nest, so it both caught the light and provided a useful reflection of her own figure.

Maggie's whiskers were droopy after her frightful experience that morning, so she decided to try a new beauty technique. She used the handle of her quill pen to curl them a bit, wrapping each whisker around the pen's surface. She had finished only one side of her face when she heard a faint scratching on the door frame just outside her nest. Anna, she thought, arriving early. Not quite the correct etiquette, to arrive early, but better to come early than late. Arriving early simply proved Anna's eagerness to be in Maggie's presence. Maggie took a deep breath and pushed open the door to see Anna jump back and crouch into herself, trembling.

"Anna," said Maggie, rather surprised. "Is that any way to greet your favorite Aunt?" Maggie had no doubt that she was the favorite of all her nieces and nephews.

"Your whiskers," stammered Anna. "Have you been frightened by something terrible?"

"Oh, for heaven's sake," replied Maggie. "Come in here and see how a sophisticated mouse prepares her toilette."

Anna scampered in. Crouched once more, she gave Maggie the benefit of a piercing stare as only a most attentive mouse can stare. It was clear that Anna was to be a quick learner.

"If you hadn't spent your whole life in a dingy cellar, you would have learned to appreciate the finer things in life," said Maggie, feeling her old self once more.

"But it's quite snug there, Auntie. And we always have a full supply of food. Why, we could live our whole lives on just the potatoes alone."

"Hmmmph," said Maggie. "Stay with me, my dear, and you will learn of true delicacies, every-thing from pheasant to ice cream."

"I'm eager to learn, Auntie. Truly I am, but per-haps I am a little young for curled whiskers. I still need the full length of my whiskers to feel move-ment in the air— to tell when someone is coming and to judge how close I am to stones or walls or chairs."

"One must sacrifice for beauty, dear heart," said Maggie as she resumed curling her whiskers. "One owes it to her admirers."

Anna tried to suppress a little squeak of laughter. "Oh, I'm afraid I have no admirers, Auntie. I have only friends."

"You shall have admirers when I am through with you, and you will start by choosing one of my frocks to wear."

Maggie enjoyed the expression of awe that transformed Anna's face. How grateful she would have been in her youth to have had the benefit of a worldly wise aunt. Anna chose a gown of crimson silk (made from Mrs. Madison's curtains) and took her place in front of the looking glass for a full view of herself in finery for the first time. Anna was amazed at looking so lovely. Why, anyone gazing on her for the first time would mistake her for a young lady, a real lady.

"You look quite pretty, dear, but wearing the right clothes is just the first step toward being refined. You must also develop the right manners and learn the art of conversation."

Maggie finished her own dressing, slipping on a cream-colored muslin gown that was dotted with violet nosegays. She topped the outfit with a matching turban.

"And now, my dear Anna, a few words of caution before we go to the party. We must be vigilant to avoid being crushed by human feet, horses' hooves, and carriage wheels. (She didn't even want to think of cats.) There will be a great deal of traffic, all manner of comings and goings on this joyful day. And since you are new to the upstairs world, I must to warn you about the evil creature that lives in this house . . . Polly, the wicked macaw. When Mr. Madison was president, a diplomat brought Polly as a gift to Dolley. The bird has haunted us ever since."

"What's a macaw?" asked Anna.

Anna's eyes widened as Maggie explained that a macaw is a kind of parrot. She went on to describe Polly's many sins, how she would screech and attack visitors (and mice) with her powerful beak and strong claws. One time, Maggie recounted, she actually bit Mr. Madison's finger all the way to the bone.

"How horrible," muttered Anna, shaking visibly.

"She has a hideous green head, a frightening gold body, and shocking blue wings. And oh, that beak." Maggie stopped to collect herself. "I cannot speak of her anymore. Just beware."

Anna seemed to have lost quite a bit of excitement over the occasion as Maggie led her down the dusty back stairs, past the dining room, and into the drawing room, which they stopped to observe in all its loveliness. This main room of the house contained examples of everything that was best from around the world, from the rich and elaborate French carpet to the red flocked wallpaper. The walls were decorated with paintings and mirrors. Four tables, one in each corner of the room, were adorned with statues. One table sported an elaborately carved chess set. In one nook was lodged a piano, and in a prominent place sat Mr. Madison's Campeachy chair, a low-slung reclining chair that relieved Mr. Madison's rheumatism.

At the sight of all the splendor, Anna regained her enthusiasm. It was the carpet that most intrigued her. The swirling design was perfect for playing hopscotch. In spite of Anna's previous fear, she jumped on the carpet, first two hind feet, then one foot, advancing across the splendid gold, red, and blue carpet, hopping, hopping, hopping. Maggie could imagine the way the carpet must feel to Anna's tiny mouse toes, toes that were more accustomed to the surface of rough bricks and splintered wood.

Although Maggie was pleased that her niece was enthralled by the carpet's beauty, she was alarmed at Anna's unguarded behavior. If Polly got a glimpse of Anna, the macaw might see her as a delicious appetizer.

"Anna," cautioned Maggie. But Anna continued to hop, seeming to be in a sort of trance, thrilled with the plush pile of the carpet. "Darling girl," Maggie said, grasping the sash of Anna's gown. "Enough," she said, pulling Anna to a stop.

The young mouse was still far from reality as she balanced on a pretty flower woven in the carpet. She leaned over to sniff it, still insensitive to Maggie's distress. Maggie firmly ushered her across the carpet and penned her niece into a corner of the room under the portraits of Mr. and Mrs. Madison.

"You must be more careful, Anna, or you'll find yourself caught in the dark beak of the devil."

She watched as Anna's eyes seemed to clear. Anna lowered her head in embarrassment. "I'm so sorry, Auntie," she said miserably. "It's just that I was having so much fun . . ."

"Good judgment must always come before fun, Anna, and today is as good a day as any to learn that warning."

Maggie was sorry she had to curb Anna's high spirits, but she was responsible for her niece's well-being. The need for safety came before anything else. She led her niece into the South Passage, adjacent to the parlor. It was a hall that led to the outside; it featured two doors to the right that were closed.

Anna's head reared up again with curiosity. "What's behind those doors, Auntie?" she asked excitedly. "More parlors?"

"Those rooms belong to Nelly Madison, Mr. Madison's mother, and we're not going to disturb her. She's a fine old lady in her nineties and enjoys her privacy."

"Does she ever come out?" asked Anna.

"Mostly people go to her. She still provides an audience for Mr. and Mrs. Madison's guests. She can hold her own in conversation, I assure you, but she prefers to keep to a quiet life of knitting and reading the Bible. And she reads the Good Book without glasses, too. Quite remarkable for a woman of her years."

Before Anna could ask to go to Mother Madison's side of the house, Maggie added firmly, "And now we will go to the party." She guided Anna to a hole beside the outside door. "We'll take the short cut to the Colonnade," she added.

The scene that greeted them on the back lawn was truly spectacular: a swirling mass of color and activity. The slaves were busily setting out platters piled high with food on tables that stretched across the lawn. Guests streamed from the mansion as well as from the woods where carriages were parked. Trees bordered the lawn, including a majestic cedar-of-Lebanon, given to Mr. Madison by the people of France. Two of the servants played popular songs on violins, adding to the general cheer.

Anna sat on her hind legs beside a column, stunned by all the activity.

"Welcome to your first Dolley Madison social event," said Maggie, coming close to Anna's ear to make herself heard. "You'll be as charmed as many before you have been."

"Good afternoon, Maggie," came a deep voice from behind her. Maggie turned to see Moses, an acquaintance from the large population of kitchen mice. He was dressed simply in brown trousers and a white shirt with large, roomy sleeves. He smiled broadly, obviously pleased to see Maggie.

Maggie observed Moses and sniffed in an indifferent fashion, thinking him beneath her in every way. Although he was a Madison mouse, he seemed to have learned nothing of refinement from residing with the Madisons. How could he have chosen such simple clothes for a party? Then she remembered that Mr. Madison always wore a plain black suit, no matter what the occasion. Hmm, but he was a genius and could wear whatever he chose. Moses was not a genius, to say the least.

"Afternoon, Moses," said Maggie, knowing she should show some courtesy. "How are things in the kitchen?"

"Everyone has been working since first light," he answered. "Baking loaves, roasting meat. And dropping food everywhere! Would you like to take a look?"

"Why ever would I want to go to that dark, damp place when I can be in the summer air, enjoying this beauty?"

She turned her eyes from him to admire the long lace tablecloths and the stacks of pretty china. She particularly admired the silver candelabras placed along the table. And then her eyes fell upon something she'd never before seen, a large cut-glass punch bowl glittering in the light. Sunbeams sent patches of brilliant light in every direction, patches containing all the colors of the rainbow. Maggie was thrilled. She couldn't keep her eyes off the sight as sunlight filtered through the leaves, providing an ever-changing show. She wanted to get closer, to catch the shifting light in her own paws, but she knew such an action might violate the first rule of mice: always avoid being seen.

She stood by Anna, her eyes fixed firmly on the crystal bowl, unaware of anything else. The bowl must be French, she mused. All of Dolley's best pieces came from France, items that had been sent by friends who visited the Continent. The bowl seemed to be speaking to her, beckoning to her. After all, who would really care if a very small mouse took a very small look at a very beautiful crystal bowl?   She would merely have to be extremely cautious, that was all. She began to make her way through the thick green grass which easily hid her advance.

The bowl had a pedestal base encircled by an ivy wreath. Maggie decided that the best plan was to climb the table and hide in the ivy ring so she could study the bowl for as long as she wished without being observed. She easily skittered up the table leg, vaguely aware that

Moses was yelling at her, but what did he know of beauty? How could he possibly understand an aristocrat's eye when confronted with an object of great splendor?

The closer she got to the bowl, the more she was struck by its radiance. She could begin to make out the carvings on its surface: glittering shapes of diamonds, circles, and fans, all catching the light and sending out multicolored images.

At last she reached the ivy wreath and settled under a large leaf, poised for further study. From such a close vantage point, she noticed that the designs were deeply cut into the glass, providing what amounted to a mouse stairway. Yes, she thought, a staircase just for her. Nothing could stop her from climbing to the top of the bowl and viewing its scalloped rim for herself. She could smell the punch's scent of rum and spices, further intoxicating her.

She adjusted her turban, which had been knocked ajar on her trip up the table leg, and started toward the pedestal. She was having some trouble balancing because of her curled whiskers, when she felt a tug on her tail.

"Stop," said Moses, who had finally caught up with her. "The humans are coming," he warned.

Maggie had no intention of letting a kitchen mouse keep her from her object of desire. She tried jerking her tail away, but Moses held firm.

"Come down, Maggie, at once."

Moses was quite a strong mouse from his heavy work of chopping wood and scavenging for food. And it's a very good thing he was, too. Just as he managed to pull the teetering Maggie off the bowl and back to the ivy wreath, two large human hands grabbed the punch bowl and lifted it high into the air.

"Let's drink a toast to Queen Dolley," said the man whose chin was covered with bushy white whiskers. "And to the country that brings forth such lovely ladies."

A loud "Hurrah" rose from the crowd, bringing Maggie back to her senses. She became aware of Moses lying by her side beneath the ivy, panting heavily with exhaustion. She was filled with shame at last. What in the world had gotten into her? If a human had seen her climbing the punch bowl, she would have been tossed into the air to fall who knew where. Her behavior was no better than

Anna's, when her niece had recklessly hopped on the French carpet.

"Are you all right, Maggie?" asked Moses, once he had recovered his breath.

She didn't know how to answer him. Her body was unharmed to be sure, but her good sense had suffered a near fatal blow. And what a dreadful example she had provided for dear little Anna.

At Home With Moses

CHAPTER FOUR

The Silver Spoon Debacle

Dear Diary,

A diary is useless unless one writes only what is true, so I must confess that I have been a very foolish mouse. I am gluing this ivy leaf to your pages to remind me that the pursuit of beauty is not a proper excuse to abandon one's wits. I had preached to little Anna about the importance of using judgment, only to forget my own lesson.

I endangered my life, Diary, just to get a closer look at a punch bowl. I know it sounds ridiculous when I describe the action so simply, but, Dear Diary, you didn't see the brilliance of its cut glass. I will remember that wondrous bowl for the rest of my life. But I can promise you that in the future, I will be more careful, even if I cannot promise I will give up my passion for beautiful things. Such a promise would mean that I would deny the very mouse I am, deep within myself. This I cannot do.

In fact, today, I am going in search of more beauty but with caution. Moses told me of a silver spoon he had rescued and hidden in his nest where it awaits my examination. Just think, Dear Diary, what a beautiful cradle that spoon would make for my future children. No mouse child has ever had such a treasure! Such a cradle would make me the best mother in the world. In the meantime, I will use it as an impressive settee.

You'll see, Diary, you'll see. This time I will be very, very careful.

* * * *

Maggie prepared herself for the trip to the kitchen. She chose a plain frock to blend in as nearly as possible to the lower-level mice: a brown dress and a white muslin turban. Since Moses had worn those colors to the party, she assumed they would be appropriate. She considered throwing a patterned shawl around her tiny shoulders, a paisley design that matched her eyes, but she quickly abandoned the idea. Simplicity had its own elegance, after all.

It was early when she set out down the stairs, pausing a moment to observe the dining room. The blue and white china was still on the mahogany table, as well as Dolley's silver flatware in the Fiddle Thread pattern, sent from France, of course. Maggie smelled a hint of ham, corn pone, and coffee in the air, but she was not tempted to search for food. She had already feasted on a kernel of corn.

She continued to slip down the stairs. She turned aside, into Mr. Madison's study where his servant, Paul Jennings, was giving him a morning shave. Mr. Madison's head was covered with a kerchief, and he wore a soft black robe. Maggie never failed to regard the old man with awe. She would have lingered awhile to regard him further in his preparations, but Paul was a vigilant observer of all things pertaining to mice. He had not proven himself an admirer. One of her brothers swore that Paul had thrown a shaving brush at him.

She set off down another set of stairs that led to the basement, and very soon she reached the entrance to the north kitchen. Maggie observed that even though the room had nothing like the abundant light of her own quarters, it was well laid out with a large fireplace where a kettle was boiling. Next to the hearth, tucked into the corner of the room, a bread oven radiated divine baking smells. Three windows shed light on the attractive pattern of bricks laid out in what was called a herringbone pattern. Instead of the bricks being set straight across as they were in Mother Madison's kitchen, they were arranged on the diagonal. Servants were busy at a long wooden table, preparing the next meal.

Maggie was looking for Moses when she heard from behind her a loud hiccup, followed by a most unattractive burp. She turned to see none other than her lamentable brother-in-law Brutus. His brown chest fur was stained with blotches of dried red wine, and he had a bleary look to his eyes. It pained her to think that this disreputable person was her dear Anna's father.

"My dear sister," he said. "Whatever brings you to these parts?"

"You are no brother of mine," Maggie answered haughtily.

"I guess you must have come because you heard the rumor that Mr. Madison is opening some of his good Madeira tonight," said Brutus. He was having trouble standing upright, swaying as if he was being blown by an unseen wind. Then he sneezed, spraying a stream of snuff on the floor close to Maggie's skirt.

"Certainly not," she said, moving away from him. "I am here at the invitation of my friend Moses. He has found something he thinks will interest me."

"Nothing more interesting than Madeira . . . my dear." Brutus chuckled as he started toward her.

Moses came running across the room to save her from the disagreeable lout.

"Step back, Brutus," said Moses. "Remember, you're in the presence of a lady."

"Lady is it?" asked Brutus with a snide expression on his messy face. "She's a mouse. No better than the rest of us."

"Come on, Maggie," said Moses, taking her paw and steering her away from Brutus and toward a large hole beside the table leg.

Moses went first. Maggie followed him down, down the tunnel that ran parallel to the kitchen wall. Many mice had spent years digging through the red clay, and the tunnel's floor and sides were worn smooth from heavy traffic. It was so wide that at least six mice could stand side by side without feeling crowded. Maggie had not visited the kitchen in a long, long time. The memories of her childhood came flooding back: all those children scrambling for food and drink; more children coming, always more; her dear father always gone, foraging for his family.

"Well, bless my soul," said a plump, tired-looking mouse. "My darling sister herself, come to visit her poor relations."

Maggie saw her sister Evangeline, leaning against the side of the run, wearing a ragged shift, and stroking her paw across a head of spiky hair.

"Hello, Evangeline," said Maggie. "You're looking . . . well fed."

"I'm a poor, poor woman," said her sister. "Destined always to serve others. Never a moment for myself." She looked Maggie up and down. "Never an opportunity for the finer things in life like my fancy Sis here. And her being from the same litter and all."

Maggie was speechless. She usually was when confronted by relatives who had abandoned the standards of the Smith-Mouse family.

"Surely you've come to give me a bit of help fixing up my nest. I've got a new batch of babies who're still pink and blind as bats . . . messing up the place. A bit of help, surely."

"I'm here to see Moses today. You know Moses."

Moses, who was standing in the shadows, clearly embarrassed, bowed his head to Evangeline.

"Oh, you've come to see Moses, is it?" said her sister. "Not me at all. Excuse me then, for expecting a moment of my sister's time. Excuse me indeed."

Maggie sometimes thought Evangeline must have been adopted. How else could she explain the difference between herself and this disheveled creature? The sight of her sister made Maggie sad, but there was nothing she could do to help. She had tried to clean Evangeline's nest dozens of times, dusting the furniture, sweeping the floor with her tail, tossing out trash, only to watch it return to the same ugly mess in a matter of hours.

"I wish you well, Evangeline, I really do," said Maggie. Then she nodded to Moses that she was ready to move on.

Evangeline stood up straight and bared her teeth at Maggie. "Miss High and Mighty," she hissed, loud enough for Maggie to hear. "The only well I wish for you . . . is a deep well that you fall into, never to return."

Maggie's stomach turned queasy as she set out in a run to catch up with Moses. She and Evangeline had never gotten along, and time had merely made things worse. But the argument made her sad and made her feel hopeless.

"Here we are," said Moses, standing at the opening of a partially hidden hole. "After you," he said to Maggie.

Maggie didn't know where Moses had learned his manners, but she was grateful for his consideration. She entered his home and was delighted to find a burning oil lamp, which cast a warm glow throughout the apartment. Moses' home was furnished quite simply: a bed made of soft fabric scraps, two black walnut shells for chairs, and a piece of kindling for a table. The most surprising thing about the room, however, was the material Moses had used to decorate his walls: sheets and sheets of newspaper.

Maggie knew that Mr. Madison received newspapers daily. It was part of the benefits of being a former president. But she had never had an interest in their content. She preferred to read letters that contained personal details.

"My goodness, Moses," she said. "Have you hung these newspapers to keep your nest cozy and warm, or do you actually read them?"

Moses looked surprised. "I read them, of course," he said. "It's the only way to keep informed of what's going on in our government.

I'm lucky that Mr. Madison has a ready supply of news."

"I can't imagine there's anything I would care to read about in Washington City. Since my Dolley left town, I'm sure it's a dull place." She sat down in one of the walnut chairs and began to rock back and forth to soothe herself after the dreadful encounter with Evangeline.

"I wouldn't be so sure about that," said Moses, going to the wall and pointing to a line of print. "It says right here that Congress has invited a very famous person to visit our country in the fall."

That caught Maggie's attention. She stopped rocking and leaned forward with anticipation.

"The Marquis de Lafayette is coming for a 'Farewell Tour' of his beloved United States, and part of his trip will include coming to Montpelier to visit the Madisons."

Maggie thought she might faint. *The* Marquis de Lafayette. Marie Joseph Paul Yves Roch Gilbert du Motier, Marquis de Lafayette! His was the most complicated name she had ever tried to memorize. And there was no one, no one in the whole world that she would rather see. Lafayette was a hero of the Revolution, a great friend of President

George Washington, and above everything, he was French nobility.

"When exactly . . ." She could hardly speak the words. "When is he coming?"

Moses studied the paper more closely, running his paw along a particular line of print. "November, I think. He will visit Mr. Jefferson at Monticello first and then come here."

November, November. She had only a few months to design and sew a new wardrobe and to freshen her nest with only the finest items. It was a well-known fact that visiting guests to Montpelier often brought with them visiting mice as well. She didn't want French lady mice to look down on her in scorn. She was nervous about being judged, but she was also eager to learn about the latest elegant styles from them. Thinking of elegance, Maggie remembered why she had come to visit Moses in the first place. The silver spoon.

"The spoon, Moses?" she reminded him. "You have a spoon for me?"

"Wouldn't you like a bite to eat first? Or perhaps a cup of tea? I made some chamomile tea especially for you."

"Very kind of you, Moses," said Maggie, "but now that I know about Lafayette's visit, I haven't a moment to spare." She observed his disappointed face and tried to think of something pleasant to say. "I wouldn't have known about his visit if it hadn't been for you. I'm ever so grateful, Moses, really I am." She smiled her sweetest smile, but still he looked somber.

Moses went to the corner of his nest, where a pile of leaves was neatly stacked. He began removing them carefully, until he revealed a beautiful spoon that he had obviously spent time polishing. It was really and truly a Madison spoon in the Fiddle Thread pattern, and Maggie fell in love with it instantly.

"I believe you're happier to see this spoon than you were to see me," he said sadly.

Maggie felt the old surge of excitement at the sight of beauty. Her racing pulse and shortness of breath reminded her of the way she had felt when she first glimpsed the crystal punch bowl. Was she in danger of being foolish again? But this was quite different, she told herself. Getting the spoon back to her nest would not involve danger. It was not as if she was throwing herself into the middle of a party. And besides, she owed it to the French mice in her future, to provide them with the finest hospitality.

"It's so lovely, Moses," she said. "Where did you find it?" She couldn't imagine the cautious Moses leaping onto the dining table to steal it. He would be much more sensible.

"The way I get almost everything. A servant dropped it."

"Oh, Moses. It's beautiful. You're an absolute prince to give it to me."

"Or a marquis, perhaps?" He smiled adorably, a fact that was lost on Maggie, who had interest only in the spoon.

Maggie knew that silver was called a precious metal, and she could understand why. It gleamed so nicely. It was so shiny that she thought she might be able to use it for a mirror, but when she leaned over the bowl of the spoon to see her reflection, the image was upside down. What a disappointment.

"If you turn it over," said Moses, "you can see yourself properly." He grasped the spoon by its slender handle and flipped it.

He was right. The back of the spoon reflected her face as well as any mirror, showing off her bright caramel-colored eyes, her black button nose, and her straight whiskers. Yes, straight whiskers. A mouse did not curl her whiskers for a visit to the kitchen.

"It's marvelous, Moses. I will treasure it forever."

"And now, maybe you'll have a cup of tea?"

Maggie closed her eyes tightly until she could feel them crinkle at the corners. She thought about how very much she wanted to take the spoon and return home immediately. She knew, however, that racing away from Moses was not the proper way to act, no matter how much she wanted to do so. After all, that was not what Dolley would have done. Mrs. Madison was greatly admired for her fashion sense, and she was even more admired for her warm personality and her gracious diplomacy. Dolley Madison was never, ever rude.

She opened her eyes again and looked at Moses' pleading eyes. He was really quite a kind friend . . . and he deserved her gratitude.

"On second thought, Moses," she said, looking him straight in the eyes. "I can't think of anything I'd rather have than a steaming cup of chamomile tea. I've loved it ever since I was a child."

She returned to her black walnut chair and arranged her skirts artfully. "Now tell me," she said, "were you born at Montpelier?"

Moses handed her the tea served in a tiny cream-colored cup. "It depends on what you mean by Montpelier. I was not born in the house, but in the tobacco fields here on the plantation. It wasn't until last year that I found my way to the kitchen."

"A field mouse?" exclaimed Maggie, forgetting her diplomacy at once. "You were raised in the out-of-doors?"

"And a fine upbringing it was, too," said Moses as he settled into his chair. His eyes took on a faraway look. He seemed unaware of Maggie's negative reaction. "Ah, the open air . . . a clear view of the mountains. We had ice skating in the winter and garden picnics in the summer. It was a fine, fine life, it was."

"But you didn't have books to study or human beings to observe."

"There were chances to learn all around me," he said. "I had lessons very early in how to hide from hawks and foxes. If I hadn't learned those things, I wouldn't be sitting with you now. And then my mother taught me other practical things: the way to split open a fig and feast on its juicy center and a clever method of pulling the strings off green beans. That sort of thing."

"So how did you ever learn to read? You can't do that from studying a cabbage leaf in the garden."

"Ah, but you can by sitting on Mr. Madison's bookshelf, listening to him recite, and later studying his texts."

"Impossible. No one could learn so much in only a year."

"But someone did, Maggie. You see him right before you."

It had taken Maggie several years to learn to read, by listening to Mrs. Madison read her letters aloud. Maggie later went over the documents herself, trying to make sense of them. Maggie was very uncomfortable with the idea that Moses might be a great deal smarter than she was. It was outrageous. It was preposterous. Whoever heard of a field mouse being more intelligent than a house mouse? It didn't bear thinking about.

Maggie stood up abruptly, so abruptly, unfortunately, that the black walnut chair was stuck to her hindquarters. She shook it loose, trying to maintain some dignity.

"I thank you very much for the tea, Moses," she said. "I'm afraid I must get back to my nest now. I've so many things to attend to. I hope you understand."

Moses was smart enough to understand that Maggie preferred talking about her accomplishments to hearing about his. He had met many mice in his lifetime who felt the same way, and that was why he was usually modest and quiet about his book learning. He had allowed himself to get too comfortable in his own home, remembering his happy life in the fields. He hoped he hadn't ruined his chances to become closer to Maggie, for he found her quite the enchantress.

Maggie stood by the spoon, trying to determine the best way to carry it back to her nest. It was an unwieldy shape. Should she pick it up by the bowl section or by the handle?

"If I might make a suggestion," said Moses, standing and slightly bowing toward Maggie. "The bowl of the spoon is the heaviest part. If you would allow me to lift that section above my head while you lift the handle, I think we can move it with the least amount of effort."

Maggie thought he made perfect sense. Of course he did. Anyone who had learned to read in only one year couldn't help but make perfect,

perfect sense. She didn't see any point to devising a different plan of her own, however, so they simply raised the spoon aloft. It was lighter than she had anticipated, and she hoped her journey home would be a speedy one. They managed to crawl through the tunnel rather efficiently. They emerged from the hole in Mr. Madison's study to enjoy a ray of glorious light. They were inching across the carpet, however, when a sound froze the blood in their tiny bodies.

They heard a "squawk." Followed by "Au secours! Au secours!" Followed by "Arrêtez. arrêtez voleur!" It was Polly, the dreaded macaw.

The bird had left her perch in the hall and was sitting before the window, preening her green and gold feathers. The ray of sunshine that Maggie had just enjoyed was the same ray of sunshine that had hit the surface of the spoon, catching Polly's attention.

"Abandon the spoon, Maggie. Run," shouted Moses, scampering toward the safety of the window curtain and letting the spoon fall to the floor with a loud clank.

But she couldn't do it. Her paws were frozen in a firm grip on the spoon handle. It was hers, rightfully hers, and no feathered menace was going to take it away. Maggie held her ground, even as she saw Polly spread her wings and flap them vigorously.

"*Au secours,*" Polly squawked again and lifted into the air.

Maggie watched Polly circle above, trembling but still unable to move. She had never been so close to the macaw, never before let herself become so vulnerable to the bird's mischief. Suddenly Polly began to dive at her, and Maggie defended herself with the spoon, swinging it wildly in the air. Polly came so close to Maggie that the mouse could feel the wind from the bird's wings and smell the faint odor of carrots on her breath. She was no match for Polly, and Maggie abandoned the spoon. She dashed toward the crimson curtain where Moses hid. Once more Polly took aim and flew at Maggie, gathering speed as she neared the mouse, coming so close that Maggie felt a tug on her fur, just as she burrowed under the curtain.

Moses welcomed her with his strong arms, and she huddled at his side, listening to the sound of arriving footsteps. Soon Mrs. Madison's maid, Sukey, entered the room and captured the boisterous macaw.

"You bad girl, causing such a ruckus," said Sukey, recovering the spoon from the floor and shaking it at Polly. "I'm taking you and your perch outside where you can't get into more trouble."

Maggie and Moses breathed freely when the room was empty once more. Maggie felt a mixture of relief and sadness. She was happy she had survived the macaw's attack but distressed that she had lost her spoon. No future cradle for her. No gleaming settee.

"It's lucky Sukey doesn't speak French," said Moses. He took Maggie's paw and led her away from the curtains. "Polly was yelling 'help' and 'stop thief.'"

"How do you know that?" asked Maggie, studying him closely.

"Oh, most of the field mice understand French. We learned from Monsieur Bizet, the gardener."

Maggie said nothing. Once more she was confronted with her ignorance. But accepting ignorance was the beginning of wisdom. She thought she'd read that somewhere. She hoped it was true.

Paris Fashion

CHAPTER FIVE

A Fashion Statement

August 1824

Dear Diary,

The strangest thing happened last evening. In the middle of the night, I woke up to the sound of music, a song coming from downstairs to the accompaniment of the Madison pianoforte. I think it was Moses singing, and I think he was singing to me. But I couldn't hear the words, just a very simple melody. That mouse is full of surprises.

I'm putting the song out of my mind now to prepare for the exciting times ahead. I am pleased to inform you, Dear Diary, that the Marquis de Lafayette is coming to Montpelier in only a few short months. I will place all my energies on making my home as attractive as possible.

I'm sure you know, Dear Diary, that the Marquis de Lafayette was a true hero of the American Revolution. When he was just a young man, not even twenty years old, he came to this country because he wanted to fight for freedom. He was with President Washington at Valley Forge and performed many acts of bravery for our country. He even convinced the French government to support us. Ah, Diary, we have so many reasons to give thanks to the Marquis.

Today, so that I can be at my best for the hero's visit, I plan to begin embellishing my garments with embroidery. I am expecting the arrival of my niece Anna, at any moment. I will be teaching her how to sew some of the more simple stitches: the outline, chain, and back stitches. She will have a good teacher. I am known for my fine needlework, and it is my duty to pass along that skill. Is that pride speaking, Dear Diary? I think it is just a statement of fact.

* * * *

Only a few moments after Maggie put away her diary, Anna arrived, wearing a green calico shift and a cream-colored apron. Her fur was a bit damp from a recent bath.

"Mama sends her regards," said Anna with a shy smile.

"And how is your dear mama?" asked Maggie, ushering her niece inside.

"Fine," she answered hesitantly. But Anna had no facility for deception.

"You don't sound convincing, dear."

"Papa has been . . . unwell," said Anna. "And several times Auntie Evangeline has asked Mama to sit with her babies while she searches for food. So Mama is a little tired these days."

"Your mother is a saint," said Maggie. "She has always borne her burdens well."

Maggie could imagine Evangeline frolicking in the garden while their sister Susan labored over her brood. A shame, but it was really none of Maggie's business.

"All right, then," said Maggie. "Let's set up for the task ahead. She went to the sewing table she had made from a scrap of wood and the finger of a soft old glove. She removed white embroidery thread, two embroidery hoops, and two needles. From her wardrobe she took two simple shifts, giving one to Anna.

"Some mice think the most difficult task is to embroider white flowers on white fabric. That may well be, but it's my belief that if you start learning to sew on undergarments, then your early mistakes will be hidden. And if you learn to master white work, then all the rest will come easily."

Maggie fastened the hoops onto each of the shifts at the hem and showed Anna how to begin with embroidering a flower stem. As they worked, Maggie considered how to entertain her niece to make the time pass more quickly.

"Have I ever told you about the clothes Mrs. Madison wore when they lived in the president's house?"

"No, you haven't, Auntie. Please tell me all about it."

"I wasn't there myself, but my grandmother told such tales, my dear. She described one outfit that stands out particularly."

Dolley was never lovelier than the night she greeted her guests wearing a rose-colored satin gown with a long train of white velvet lined with lavender satin and edged with the finest lace. Her turban was in matching white velvet, adorned with white ostrich feather tips. At the very front of the turban was a crown embroidered in gold thread.

"Oh, Auntie," said Anna. "Can you teach me to embroider a gold crown?"

"All in good time, my dear."

"Please tell me more!"

"I'll make a bargain with you," said Maggie. "If you are a good, industrious girl, and embroider four stems and four flowers without fault, I'll take you to see the clothes in Mrs. Madison's quarters."

Nothing Maggie could have said would have provided a better motivation for young Anna. She set to her task without asking any more questions and had finished her flowers before thirty minutes had passed. Maggie made sure Anna stowed her sewing materials neatly in the table before they set off on their newest adventure.

After they slipped into Dolley's chambers, Anna admired the four-poster bed with its elegant crimson hangings, but what she really wanted to see were the gowns and the jewelry. The two mice climbed up the wardrobe chest and together pushed open the lid of Dolley's jewelry box.

"Ahhh," said Anna upon seeing the treasure inside.

Even Maggie, who had seen inside the jewelry box many times, responded, "Oooh."

Nestled inside were gold necklaces and bracelets, fancy brooches, and a silver crown. A pair of glistening emerald earrings was designed in the shape of "M." Curled in one of the corners was the most treasured ornament of all . . . a strand of finest pearls.

Maggie watched as Anna suddenly hopped into the box and rubbed her furry face against the surface of one of the pearls. Maggie understood the impulse since she had done the same thing many times. Then Anna surprised her by suddenly licking the pearl, as if she thought it might taste of sweet cream and sugar.

"Be careful," Maggie said to Anna. "We mustn't hurt Mrs. Madison's pearls. They are her pride and joy and the most expensive jewels she owns. Each one is perfectly matched with the others."

Anna climbed over the jewels and out of the box. She helped her aunt close the lid and followed Maggie obediently to the clothespress where, as luck would have it, one of Dolley's drawers was open, a gown spilling over the side. It was made of yellow satin, embroidered all over with butterflies, each one a different design. Maggie and Anna sat side by side, admiring the splendid sight. One butterfly would be pictured in flight, its wings spread wide. The next one would show a butterfly sitting on a flower.

"You see, Anna, how embroidery can be raised to a high art," said Maggie. No one could have disputed her while looking at such a dress, not even the Marquis de Lafayette himself.

"*Excuse-moi,*" said a voice out of nowhere.

Maggie grabbed Anna's paw and pulled her into one of Dolley's ivory satin slippers that sat near the clothespress.

"*Parlez-vous Français?*" the voice continued. It was clearly not one of the house servants. None of them spoke French at Montpelier.

"*Pardonnez,*" said the voice. "I was hoping to find someone educated to speak with," it continued in English.

In spite of her fear, Maggie didn't like that suggestion that she was uneducated, no matter who was speaking.

"And I beg your pardon," she said to the unseen speaker as she climbed out of the slipper and marched to the center of room. "At least I'm not afraid to show myself. Who are you? Come out at once!"

"I am Josette," said the voice. "And unfortunately, I cannot move from my place here on the top of this wardrobe."

Maggie had been so focused on looking at the yellow butterfly gown that she hadn't bothered to look anywhere else. Now she surveyed the clothespress. Sure enough, there on the top was a doll with a china head, a pink satin lace-trimmed dress and little china hands that stuck out from her sleeves. Her cheeks were painted with bright pink circles and black curls poked from beneath a simple turban. She had never seen a talking doll before and was truly astonished.

Maggie introduced both herself and Anna who had joined her.

"I am so forlorn," said the doll. She went on to explain that a guest had brought her to Montpelier as a house gift, but Mrs. Madison had put her on the clothespress and forgotten all about her.

"She says she will save me for visiting children to play with. Imagine the insult! *Mon Dieu.*"

"I'm sure the children will treat you gently," said Maggie, trying to be encouraging.

"I am not a plaything!" exclaimed Josette. "I am a fashion doll. I demonstrate the finest style of the day. You see the fabric of my dress? It is the latest from Paris. The neckline you see here is favored by the empress herself."

"I think Mrs. Madison chooses her styles from a magazine. *Akermann's Repository,*" said Maggie.

"A magazine! How can some drawing in a magazine compare to the experience of touching the fabric oneself? The lace on my bodice is the finest from Brussels. A magazine cannot show such detail. Come up and see for yourself."

Maggie thought it extraordinary good luck to meet a real French fashion doll just before the Marquis's visit, so she scampered up the clothespress until she was sitting in front of Josette.

"It is a terrible, terrible thing," said the doll dramatically, "to be alone and so far from home."

"I imagine so," replied Maggie, who could imagine no such thing. Her whole world was Montpelier and always would be.

"I was born in a famous French fashion house," continued Josette, "surrounded by the most elaborate fabrics and trimmings in the whole world. Royalty came to our atelier . . . the most distinguished ladies on the continent. And then to be sent here, unappreciated, abandoned. Waiting for the attention of some silly child who will probably pull off my head."

"I think I can help you," said Maggie, her eyes sparkling in anticipation of what she was going to say.

"Impossible," said Josette. "You are a mouse. *Une souris!*"

"It's true, I am a mouse," said Maggie, "but I can do things you can't do. I can move, most importantly. And I happen to know that very soon we are expecting a visit from the Marquis de Lafayette. And while he is here, it should be possible for me to hide you in his luggage so that when he returns to France, you will return as well."

Josette was speechless. Maggie studied her face, which showed no expression since her features were merely painted on china. Maggie imagined the doll would be crying with joy if such a thing were possible.

"You would do this thing for me?" asked Josette, her voice quavering with emotion.

"I might need help from my friends, but I'm sure we could do it. The marquis will be staying in the large bedroom just around the corner from my nest. We should be able to reach his luggage with ease."

"Ah," said Josette with a faraway look in her eyes. Of course, there was always a faraway look in her eyes.

"But what can I do for you?" asked Josette.

It was the question Maggie had been hoping for. "I need your advice on fashion," said Maggie. "I want to be the equal of any mouse in the marquis's traveling entourage."

"Stand up," said Josette. "Here in front of me so I can get a good look."

Maggie stood as straight as she could, stiffened her spine, and waited for Josette's assessment.

"We will start the transformation with close attention to the colors you should use," said Josette. "Peach, close to your face, I think. Yes, peach is just the right choice to bring out your natural beauty."

Maggie could feel herself blush. She hoped she blushed with a peachy tone.

Friends Unite

CHAPTER SIX

The Letter Dilemma

September 1824

Dear Diary,

I have been in such a flurry of activity the past few days that I have forgotten you entirely. Please accept my apologies. I have a new fashion consultant, a doll named Josette, who has kept me quite busy. She knows more than I have ever dreamed about creating the proper look. "Details," she commands. "Perfection is all in the details."

For instance, she insisted that I must have plumage for my turbans, so I searched the house and extracted some nice goose feathers from one of the bed pillows. My really inspired trophy, however, came from the dining room: a peacock feather. Mrs. Madison has so many of them arranged in a vase—I don't think she will miss the one I took.

I think at this time, Dear Diary, I should explain to you why Mrs. Madison worked so diligently on becoming a fashion leader while she was living in Washington City. As you know, the United States is a very young nation, far younger . . . well, far younger than any other country. And the European ambassadors and their wives were quite ready to look down on us as country bumpkins.

It was, therefore, very important that my Dolley put these foreigners in their place by demonstrating that although we are a young country, we are a young country with style and not to be looked down upon. She not only dressed the part of a great lady, but she also decorated the president's mansion in the most tasteful way. That is why I must keep up my part as well, so that any European mice who might visit will not look down on me. I must be a credit to my country!

But I admit, Dear Diary, that I am having trouble with the notion of a train attached to my dress. Josette says it is absolutely necessary to have one. The truth is, a train might look perfectly fine on a human with two legs, but a mouse who must walk on four legs runs the risk of getting into quite a tangle.

* * * *

Maggie was interrupted by a sharp knocking on her door. The noise was loud and insistent, something she would have liked to ignore, but it was impossible. She put down her pen, carefully stored her diary, and went to see who was causing the disturbance.

There was Moses in his customary white shirt and tan breeches, but with a most uncustomary fire in his eyes. It was clear to Maggie that this was no ordinary social call.

"You must come quickly," he said. "Mrs. Madison needs you."

Maggie couldn't imagine any circumstance in which Mrs. Madison might need her, but she was extremely flattered nonetheless.

"Let me get my shawl," she replied. The fall mornings were bringing a touch of chill to the air, and the downstairs was much draftier than Maggie's comfortable upstairs nest.

"Hurry," said Moses. "You need to hear what she's discussing with Mr. Madison."

Maggie pulled a brown shawl from a knob on the wall, knowing it wasn't her best color, but also knowing it would blend in well with the floor. She followed Moses down the stairs, past two of the servants who were passing in the hall passage, and into Mr. Madison's study. Dolley was wearing a simple green frock and a white cap while Mr. Madison was dressed in his usual black suit. Mrs. Madison was waving a letter in her right hand.

"I'm not going to do it," she said. "I am a private person who deserves her privacy."

"You're hardly a private person, my dear," said Mr. Madison gently. "Why, I think you were the most notable person in my administration."

"I was elected to no office. You appointed me to no office. No one has the right to ask for copies of my letters. They belong to me."

"And you belong to history," he said.

"Well, I don't want to make them public. And that's final."

Maggie had never seen Mrs. Madison so agitated. Dolley paced the carpet, crumpling the letter in her hand.

"My letters were for my friends and family, not for the eyes of strangers. How could they possibly interest anyone else?" she asked.

"Surely you want to share the letter you wrote to your sister Lucy on the day the British attacked Washington. That story belongs to history."

"Hmmph," said Dolley. "Maybe I could allow that one letter to be published, but my days of public life are over."

"My dear," said Mr. Madison, "perhaps you should give this matter more thought. I appreciate your desire for privacy, but I also know your devotion to your country."

"This has nothing to do with feelings for my country," she replied with frustration. "I wish the letters had been torn to bits by mice. That would solve everything," she added, and promptly left the room.

Maggie looked at Moses in amazement. It was as if her dear Dolley had been speaking directly to her. Maggie had been given an important task, and she had no intention of failing.

The job of destroying Dolley's letters was too large for Maggie to carry out alone, even with the help of Moses. So late that night in the kitchen, Moses assembled his many friends to participate in the difficult endeavor. The servants, finished with their cooking duties, had retired to their separate houses outside the mansion, leaving the basement entirely to the mice. The hearth fire still smoldered, casting an eerie light on the mouse gathering.

Maggie saw Brutus in the crowd right away, weaving among the mice in his regular state of drunkenness. Her sister Susan and her niece Anna were in the front row, eager to help. And of course Evangeline was there too, always ready for a chance of excitement whether for good or ill. Most of the mice, however, were strangers to Maggie, and she had to depend on Moses for their reliability.

"Thank you for coming," said Maggie to the eager mice before her. "We have a very important assignment this evening."

Maggie had to stop talking for a moment to clear her throat. She was not used to speaking in public and only the fact that Dolley had asked for her efforts gave her the strength to continue.

"Mrs. Madison has requested our help in destroying her letters," she explained. "They are stored in a trunk just outside her bedroom door. Our job is to open that trunk, remove the letters, and nibble them until nothing remains that anyone could read."

"Shucks," said Brutus. "I couldn't read anything to begin with."

Maggie waited for the laughing to stop before she continued. "Here's the important thing," she said. "I must read each letter before you destroy it, because there is one important letter we must save."

"What you're suggesting could take all night," said Evangeline, "Can't you read them by yourself, and we can get around to eating them later?"

"I agree this process will take time," said Maggie, "But helping Mrs. Madison is the most important thing any of us could be doing this evening."

"I don't know about that," said Evangeline. "I've got my little ones to think of. They'll be crying for their mother. Not that you'd know anything about that. You in your fine nest upstairs."

"The Madisons have given us a perfect home," Maggie continued, ignoring her, "with warm fires and plenty of food."

"And wine," said Brutus. "Don't forget that."

"Now we have the opportunity to give back to our benefactors."

"The paper and glue will be tasty too," added Moses encouragingly. "We'll all get a benefit as well."

Although Evangeline still had a surly expression on her face, all the other mice looked appropriately determined to achieve the task, and almost one hundred mice followed Maggie and Moses as they marched up the stairs and filed down the hall to Dolley's bedroom.

Sure enough, the trunk was lodged on the floor, just outside the room, but sadly with the lid firmly closed.

"Now what do we do, Auntie?" asked Anna. The mice behind her were similarly discouraged as to how they might open the trunk which loomed above them in the darkness. They began chattering loudly.

"Shhhh," said Moses. "We'll form a mouse pyramid," he commanded. "We'll start with a base of twenty mice and keep climbing on our brothers' shoulders until we reach the latch."

"What if it's locked?" asked Anna. "She wants to keep her letters private, after all."

"We'll deal with that if we have to, but first we press on."

Moses organized the pyramid, stationing every mouse as necessary and helping each one into place. When the pyramid was almost up to the latch, he began his own ascent, crawling up the backs of the others as if he were climbing a ladder. When he was finally at the top, he pushed as hard as he could on the latch, his little face turning as red as Mrs. Madison's curtains. Slowly he felt it ease open and called for his friends to push him higher. Each mouse responded by pushing the mouse above him a little harder until Moses shoved the trunk open and the lid fell back with a loud thud. The motion sent the mice tumbling into a pile of gray and brown bodies, accompanied by a goodly amount of squealing.

"Be quiet," said Moses as he lay in the middle of his squiggling, jiggling friends. "Be quiet *now*," he added. Although Moses had torn a patch of fur from his right paw, his mission had been completed. Now the mice could climb into the trunk with ease and retrieve the letters.

"I need five volunteers," said Maggie to the group. "We'll climb into the trunk and sort the letters. Then we'll throw down the ones that need to be destroyed."

Several mice raised their paws, and Maggie chose the five strongest to join her, including Moses, of course. If there was anyone she could count on, it was Moses.

"What about me?" asked Susan, looking disappointed.

"And me?" added Evangeline, looking angry.

"Susan," said Maggie, "you will organize the demolition crew here on the ground. And Evangeline." Maggie paused. "I can't think of anyone who can destroy things any better than you."

Maggie led her team of five brave mice up the steep side of the trunk until they reached the top. As she surveyed the huge pile of letters, she felt her courage waver. How could they possibly eliminate this mountain of paper in one night of work?

"We will take it one letter at a time," said Moses, reading her mind. "Just one letter at a time," he repeated, patting Maggie on the shoulder.

"The letter we're looking for," said Maggie, "should be addressed to Dolley's sister Lucy. That's Lucy Payne Washington Todd."

For the first time, she was grateful for Moses' ability to read, even if he *had* learned more quickly than she. She turned to her team.

"Moses and I will jump in to read the letters' addresses. We'll hand you the ones that need to be destroyed, and you will toss them to our friends below."

They nodded solemnly, and soon the plan became reality with a great flurry of tossing and chewing.

After an hour Maggie's eyes became bleary. She signaled to Moses and the others to take a break. She leaned against the inside of the trunk and wiped her eyes with her paws.

"I wish Mrs. Madison didn't have so many, many friends," she sighed.

"I'm thinking," said Moses, "that maybe we shouldn't destroy all of these letters." He put his forearm on her shoulder and drew her near him. Maggie was too tired to resist. In fact, she rather liked the feeling of his warm side against hers. It was comforting.

"Mrs. Madison may change her mind about wanting the letters torn up," he said. "She may decide they should be preserved after all."

"It's too late for that," said Maggie. "We must have gone through more than a hundred letters already."

"I think we should take a look at how our troops on the floor are managing," said Moses. "If we're tired, they must be as well."

They climbed to the rim of the trunk and surveyed a deplorable scene below. Some of the letters had been turned into a smattering of white dust on the wooden floor while other letters lay in various stages of destruction. What was most distressing was the dwindling number of worker mice: no more than ten remained. Evangeline was nowhere to be seen. Susan had given her leadership role to Anna while she tried to revive the unconscious Brutus. He lay flat on his back with the corner of an envelope clamped between his jaws.

"Oh dear," said Maggie, contemplating the messy scene below. "It seems as if we have surely bitten off more than we can chew."

"But we've made a brave start," said Moses. "Look how much we've accomplished."

"I'm afraid I didn't think this through properly," said Maggie. "What will the Madisons do when they see this wreckage in the morning?"

70

"It doesn't help to think about that," said Moses. "We still have time to find the letter to Mrs. Madison's sister."

Maggie and Moses dismissed all the others and returned to the trunk, sifting through the letters until they finally found what they were looking for: the letter written to Lucy ten years before. The date was August 23, 1814, written at the height of the war with Britain when foreign soldiers were advancing on Washington City. Both Maggie and Moses read eagerly.

The letter told the story of what happened on that fateful day when President Madison was out on the battlefield with his generals while Dolley remained at home. She had received a note from him, instructing her to be ready to leave their house at a moment's notice. While she waited for a signal, she had loaded the cabinet papers into trunks. When she paused to take out her spyglass to look for any signs of Mr. Madison's arrival, all she saw were wandering soldiers, too confused to fight, and citizens leaving the city by the droves.

At three o'clock, with cannon booming in the distance, Dolley and her servants filled a wagon with silver objects and other valuables in anticipation of departing. But still she refused to leave. There was one job remaining before she could abandon the house. She had to protect the famous painting of General George Washington. She instructed the servants to unscrew the painting from the wall, and when it could not be removed quickly, she ordered the frame to be broken and the canvas removed. The general had defeated the British once. Thanks to Mrs. Madison, he would not have to surrender to them on this occasion either.

Maggie read the last words of the letter aloud. "When I shall again write you or where I shall be tomorrow, I cannot tell!!"

As Maggie folded the letter to return it to the envelope, she had tears in her eyes. To think that her Dolley had been in such danger! Mrs. Madison had stayed in the house until the last possible moment, saving the famous painting, valuable papers, and what personal items she could. But what if the British had captured her? It was bad enough that they later set fire to the president's house, but what if Dolley had been a prisoner? It was too much to even think of.

"I had never heard that story," said Moses solemnly. "This is certainly a letter worth saving. It's a story for the history books."

Maggie nodded but said nothing more. There are some thoughts too deep for words.

A Dreadful Note

CHAPTER SEVEN

The Aftermath

Dear Diary,

The entire household is in an uproar since they found the remains of letters we destroyed last night . . . at Mrs. Madison's request, of course. The servants are running about with brooms, sweeping scraps of paper into piles, searching the baseboards for holes where mice might have hidden. They truth is, they will never find us. We can wedge into the tiniest of openings and disappear. The disturbance has even extended to Mother Madison's side of the house. I overheard her servant, Sawney, say that she was quite upset over a mouse population that can cause such damage in an evening.

What will happen next, Dear Diary, I cannot predict. But I will be vigilant. I hereby paste upon this page a fragment of one of Dolley's letters as a testament to my devotion. And now I must be off to discover the latest news.

* * * *

Maggie glued the piece of paper to her diary and closed the book. She set about dressing in her darkest, dreariest outfit, one that would allow her to skitter along the walls unnoticed. After looking both left and right at her door, she made her way down into the parlor where the Madisons often went to confer about important matters. She searched the room for a suitable hiding place when her eyes fell on the chessboard. "Aha," she thought. No one would notice her there. She stealthily climbed the table and huddled next to the red queen.

Sure enough, in only a few moments, the Madisons entered the room, Dolley with the dreaded macaw sitting on her shoulder. At the sight of that awful bird, rotating its head in surveillance, Maggie turned to stone.

"What will we do, Jemmy?" asked Dolley, sitting down on a sofa. "The marquis will be visiting soon, and we can't let him think we live like savages."

"Now my dear," said Mr. Madison, settling into his Campeachy chair, "I dare say every house in France has its resident mouse."

"One mouse, perhaps, but we apparently have a regiment," said Dolley. Each of her cheeks was flushed, giving her a complexion quite like that of the doll Josette.

"*Quelle horreur*," cried Polly, who followed those words with a disarming squawk.

"I can just imagine sitting down to my table with the finest foods, only to be assaulted by a host of rodents!"

"Rodents?" thought Maggie. Such a harsh word from her precious Dolley. If only Maggie could introduce herself to Mrs. Madison, she was sure Dolley would see mice in a kinder light. But this was not the time to do so. This was the time to hide and remain as still as possible. But in spite of herself, Maggie found the need to press even closer to the chess piece.

"If you can devise a constitution, serve as the country's secretary of state, run the nation as president for eight years . . . even win a war with England, surely, Jemmy, you can come up with a way of eliminating dirty mice."

Maggie was brokenhearted. Dirty indeed.

"*C'est terrible*," squawked Polly.

Maggie could have sworn there was a smile on the macaw's beak.

"I'll speak to Mother about it," said Mr. Madison with a deep and heavy sigh.

"Your mother?" Dolley asked with surprise. "Why ever would you bother her?"

"She's lived in this house for more years than we have, after all. I'm sure she's dealt with this problem in the past."

"I'd ask her about knitting or quotes from the Bible, but I would not disturb her on the subject of mice."

"We'll see, dearest. We'll see," he answered, getting to his feet with some difficulty. "Catching the mice will be like playing a chess game. We must develop a strategy to win."

Maggie froze at the sound of the word *chess*. What if they looked at the board! But much to her relief, Dolley stood as well and followed Mr. Madison out of the room. Only Polly's eyes were focused on her as the macaw looked over Mrs. Madison's shoulder. Maggie wondered if the bird was only biding her time.

* * * *

Later that day Maggie found Mr. Madison in deep concentration at his desk in the study. She climbed the bookshelves to her accustomed hiding place where she could see what he was writing. Unfortunately, he was leaning over the paper in such a way that blocked her view.

She settled down to wait until he shifted his position. She had made up her mind that morning, after overhearing the Madisons' conversation, to trail Mr. Madison closely. She had been following him on his way to Mother Madison's chambers, when Anna had interrupted her with the latest family emergency. Evangeline had abandoned her brood, leaving Anna's mother to care for a nest full of squalling babies. In addition to that calamity, no one had been able to awaken Brutus from his deep sleep that morning, and they feared he was in a coma.

Maggie had abandoned her job of tracking Mr. Madison and gone to help her family. She managed to find Evangeline in one of the vegetable barrels where she was eating her way through a large potato. Maggie shamed her sister into returning to collect her children from Susan. Then she splashed Brutus with the cold water she had collected in a broken bottle, and he sputtered his way back to consciousness. Maggie wondered if every family was so plagued with problems.

With the emergencies taken care of, she was actually enjoying her bit of rest, warm and snug against the leather spine of a book. Suddenly Mr. Madison stood and left the room for no apparent reason. It seemed the perfect occasion for Maggie to read his note, so she ran quickly down the shelves and over to his desk. This is what she read:

To Paul
I have consulted with my mother this morning, on the subject of mice. She agrees that we need to address the problem.
Mother would like for you to find a cat.

For a moment Maggie was quite paralyzed. From the fur on the top of her head to the skin at the tip of her tail, she could move nothing. Not even her whiskers vibrated. If there was one word in the English language that most terrified her, it was the word CAT. The presence of a macaw was a danger. The presence of a cat was a catastrophe. Her head started spinning at the memory of being chased by the big orange cat.

She had to get hold of herself. And she had to act fast before Mr. Madison returned. It was imperative that she destroy the note, that much was clear. Maggie managed to shake her shoulders, trying to restore her ability to move. Slowly, very slowly, much more slowly than she would have wished, she began to recover. Instead of being frozen, however, she began to tremble in fear at the thought of cats. She had seen them out by the barns, in the garden, and skulking near the servants' quarters, but never, ever in the house. How she hated their sneaking ways, their stalking manner, their pouncing action. Cats were a dreadful foe, and she must keep them away at all costs. She must destroy the note.

Although that message was written on an average-sized piece of paper, from a mouse's point of view it was huge. Maggie tried to roll it up, starting at one corner, but when she had rolled it for about two inches, it would go no further and began to unroll itself, trapping Maggie beneath the parchment.

She decided that the thing to do was to push the paper off the desk. Once it was on the floor, she could drag it back to her nest. Then perhaps Mr. Madison would forget all about the message when he returned. Maggie grabbed the paper with her forepaws and pushed it steadily, advancing toward the edge of the desk. Using all her strength, she gave the note one last powerful push, and it fluttered to the floor. Unfortunately, the notepaper took Mr. Madison's inkwell with it as well, sending the brass container thudding to the floor and splashing a large amount of ink across the floorboards.

Maggie was appalled. Mr. Madison couldn't help but notice his precious inkwell on the floor. He would surely be aware something had happened in his absence. She didn't have long to worry about the inkwell, however, because something even worse happened. The sound of the loud thump had caught someone else's attention—Polly the macaw.

The bird swooped into the room, a rainbow of color in the air: her golden breast, her blue wings, her green head, all spelled danger. Maggie could see Polly's bright black eye trained solely on herself. The bird opened her powerful beak wide enough for Maggie to see the scaly tongue, and Polly started toward her. The little mouse responded by diving under Mr. Madison's note for protection.

The loud sound of Polly's squawking and the sound of ripping paper tortured Maggie's ears. She felt her protective covering being torn and lifted from her body. All that remained was a small fragment of paper Maggie had clutched in her paws. Polly continued her horrible flapping of wings, and then Maggie heard footsteps coming. She dived for the nearest opening in the base-board, dragging the paper with her.

Mr. Madison entered the room to the sight of Polly, still circling above with the incriminating note in her mouth.

"Bad bird," said Mr. Madison. He managed to catch one of Polly's legs and pull her toward him. "Look at what a mess you've made."

"*Je suis innocent,*" squawked the macaw, dropping the note from her beak in the process of speaking.

"Innocent?" asked Mr. Madison, seizing the shredded paper. "I think not," he said, waving the note in Polly's face. "You're going outside now, my dear girl," said Mr. Madison. "I've had enough of your tricks for one day."

He left the room with Polly in one hand and the note in the other. After a few moments, Maggie dared to crawl into the study once more. She spread the remaining scrap of paper across the floor to see what words remained: "Mother would . . ." She hoped with all her mouse heart that, in fact, mother wouldn't, wouldn't ever find a cat.

Sophisticated Visitors

CHAPTER EIGHT

At Last

November 15, 1824

Dear Diary,

The day has finally come for the arrival of General Lafayette. A few weeks ago, Mr. Madison went to join him, first at Mr. Jefferson's home, Monticello, and then for a dinner at the University of Virginia in Charlottesville. Mr. Madison sent a letter describing the marquis in these words: "He is in fine health and spirits, but so much increased in bulk and changed in aspect that I should not have known him." So much for the rich quality of French foods. Mr. Madison tells of four hundred dinner guests seated under the domed ceiling of the rotunda at the university. What a sight that must have been!

Mrs. Madison stayed here to prepare for the marquis's visit. You cannot imagine, Dear Diary, such a flurry of activity as we have seen. Every surface has been dusted.

Every piece of silver has been shined. The china has been inspected for nicks or cracks. For days Mrs. Madison has been unable to keep still, moving through every room, checking the mirrors for smudges and straightening the paintings on the walls. The servants have aired the mattress in the large bedroom and covered it with our finest sheets. The other bedrooms have been similarly prepared. Thank heavens, she appears to have forgotten all about mice. Mr. Madison has returned now and watches the preparations with an amused smile.

Moses tells me the preparations in the kitchen have been just as elaborate. I offered to make him a new suit of clothes for the upcoming occasion, but he only laughed. I did not consider that a proper way to answer what I considered to be a generous offer, but what can you expect from a kitchen mouse?

And most important of all, Mr. and Mrs. Madison are even now on the front porch, Dolley with her spyglass trained on the road that approaches Montpelier. He is coming. He is coming at last.

* * * *

Maggie perched on the window ledge in "her" upstairs bedroom, shaking with excitement. She was dressed in her finest new garment, a peach satin dress with Empire neckline and long, fitted sleeves. A matching turban with plumes finished her attire. It had no train, however. Maggie had held firm about having no train, and Josette had reluctantly agreed.

Even before she saw any of the marquis's entourage, she heard the sound of a bugle and saw hundreds of Orange County citizens who had gathered to pay their respects to the general. They formed in lines on each side of the drive, the ladies waving their white handkerchiefs. First came a small group of Albemarle Lafayette Guards (the majority of their number having escorted the general only as far as the Gordonsville Circle). Next came a landau, an elaborate carriage, holding the general, Mr. Madison, and Mr. Jefferson's grandson, among others. Two more carriages followed with the marquis's son, George Washington Lafayette, his secretary, Auguste Levasseur, other notables, and the servants. The last vehicle was a very large covered wagon that held everyone's luggage.

Maggie watched as the general climbed from the coach and removed his black top hat to greet Mrs. Madison. He was dressed in a black suit and white shirt that featured a standing collar. A white cravat encircled his neck and tied in a soft bow under his chin. A long brown coat with a fur collar completed his attire.

Maggie observed that although the marquis did not have the slender figure of a young man, he was by no means as portly as she had feared from Mr. Madison's description. He still possessed a full head of dark brown hair which curled across his forehead, framing his face. A fine figure of a man. Maggie was not disappointed in any way.

In short order, the marquis kissed Dolley's hand, waved to the crowd, and the entire traveling party left the vehicles and entered the house. Maggie knew that servants would soon bring the marquis's luggage to his bedroom, so she jumped from the window ledge and hurried to the guest bedroom to await its arrival.

In just a few moments, Paul Jennings entered the large bedroom, followed by two Frenchmen who carried large trunks which they slung to the floor. The floorboards shook, making Maggie feel as if she was experiencing a little earthquake.

"*Eh bien*," said the larger of the two men, wiping his hands with satisfaction. The other set about opening the trunks, fluffing the clothes to give them air. Maggie expected more servants to come along soon to brush and hang the marquis's clothes in the wardrobe.

"Would you like something to drink?" Paul asked. He used his hands to gesture putting a glass to his lips.

"*Mais oui,*" said the first man, a strong burly fellow. "Yes, of course," he added with a strong foreign accent.

The two men followed Paul out of the room and down the stairs, leaving Maggie alone to examine the marquis's luggage. She crept slowly across the floor, sniffing all the way, searching for a smell that hinted of France. She found nothing particularly different in the smell of the leather bag. Then she picked up a floral scent, a perfume with the odor of lilacs. Could it be that the marquis used perfume?

She did not have long to ponder this question when she discovered the real origins of the wonderful smell. Two lady mice wriggled themselves from the folded clothing and stood breathing deeply, enjoying the fresh air. Shortly they began chattering between themselves, presumably in French, since Maggie couldn't understand anything they said. But one thing she could understand very well. Their dresses were cut quite differently from what Josette had told her was the latest style. Instead of being designed with a high Empire waist, their waists were fitted tightly at the natural waistline. Furthermore, their sleeves were large and their skirts were full. Instead of turbans, they wore large brimmed hats decorated with flowing ribbons. In short, their costumes were just the opposite of Maggie's.

Maggie approached the trunk to welcome her new guests.

"Excuse me," she said politely.

They stopped speaking abruptly and turned to observe her. Maggie thought she had never seen such an arrogant expression on anyone's face.

"Que'est-ce que c'est?" asked the one in lavender, pointing to Maggie. The one in blue joined her in a disapproving stare.

"Allow me to introduce myself. I am Maggie Smith-Mouse. I'm pleased to welcome you to Montpelier."

"Parlez-vous Français?" asked the lavender mouse in a chilling tone.

Maggie understood their meaning from the word Français. "No, I'm afraid I don't speak French," she answered.

"Ah," came another voice from inside the trunk. "How very fortunate. Now we will have a chance to practice our English."

Out popped the most handsome, elegant, debonair mouse Maggie had ever seen. Well, perhaps debonair was not a word that came to Maggie's mind because no man or mouse she had ever known or seen was as suave or urbane as this mouse.

He stood on the trunk's rim, bowed to Maggie, and nonchalantly made his way down the side of the luggage until he presented himself in front of her, his black top hat in his paw.

"I am Philippe." He pronounced his name "Feeleep," in a low, resonant voice. "I am so honored to meet such a beautiful lady as yourself."

Maggie was hypnotized. Fortunately Philippe continued to talk as he strolled across the room, and she was spared the embarrassment of searching for a response. She admired his emerald velvet cutaway coat, double breasted and decorated with two rows of gold buttons. His long, pearl-gray trousers were full through the hips, tapering to the ankles. They were held in place by straps fastened under his black square-toed shoes.

"Dear lady," he continued, "I want to know everything about your beautiful country." He stopped and turned toward her. "And of course," he added with a charming smile, "everything about your beautiful self as well."

"Pay no attention to him," said the mouse dressed in lavender. "You'll never hear *un mot sensible* from his mouth. I am Francine, by the way, and I have but learned the *difficile* way."

"Philippe is my brother," added Marie, the mouse in blue. "I know very well how he is full of the nonsense."

Philippe only smiled. "Judge for yourself, Mademoiselle. That is all I can ask."

Maggie tried not to blush as she spoke. "It is a great honor to welcome you, all of you, to my home, Montpelier."

"Ah yes. Montpelier," said Philippe. "A French name entirely. How *charmant*."

Maggie had no idea what he was talking about. Montpelier was just Montpelier to her. She had no idea if the name had a French origin.

Philippe continued to survey the room. "I like the peach color of the walls, just the color of your lovely dress, of course. A lovely room. Entirely suitable. For us and the marquis."

Francine and Marie, tired of standing in the traveling trunk, joined Maggie and Philippe on the floor.

"I am feeling quite fatigued from our trip. Is it possible to find something to drink?" asked Francine, shaking her skirts to remove the wrinkles. "*Tres, tres fatigue*," she added, bringing her forepaw to her brow.

"I can still hear that horrid cheering and shouting in my ears. You Americans are a rowdy lot," said Marie.

"It is but a tiny price to pay for traveling with a hero, ladies," said Philippe. "I consider us blessed." He gave Maggie a warm smile.

"The kitchen is just downstairs," said Maggie. "We can find something to drink there." She avoided using the word *basement*, for fear of hearing further complaints from the French ladies. Soon enough she would have to face their scorn. If they had thought her clothes were contemptible, they would surely be aghast at Moses' informal breeches and his tradesman shirt. She could only hope that Evangeline and Brutus would stay out of sight.

As they moved down the stairs, Maggie could hear a thunder of conversation booming from the parlor. Occasionally she could make out Dolley's pretty laughter above the male voices. She was glad things seemed to be progressing much better in the party of humans than in the party of mice. She led her group close to the dining room walls while a multitude of servants passed through the room with trays of food.

"Beware of ending up under their feet," Maggie warned as she shepherded the little flock down the final flight of stairs to the kitchen.

"*Mon Dieu*," said Francine as she observed the kitchen's low ceiling and the swarm of activity. "We shall all perish."

"This way," said Maggie. "Be quick about it."

"*Vite, vite*! Hurry, hurry!" added Marie as they ran after Maggie to the welcoming hole in the wall under the long table. Once safely inside the tunnel, they all took deep breaths of air, and the French ladies leaned against the red clay walls to recover.

"Watch out," said Maggie. "That clay can stain your fine clothes."

Francine looked at the dirty smudge on her shoulder and shuddered. "Such a country!" she said. "I do not understand why the marquis chose to return."

"*Bon jour, belles Desmoiselles. Bon jour, Monsieur.*" It was Moses, holding a candle and bowing to the French visitors. He was dressed in his usual farmhand clothes, but to Maggie's astonishment, the French ladies did not seem to be offended. In fact, they seemed to be very impressed.

"*Ah Monsieur, enfin un gentleman.*"

Although Maggie didn't understand French, she could have sworn they called Moses a gentleman.

"*Vous parlez Français, Monsieur?*"

"I do," replied Moses. "I had the good fortune to learn French from Mr. Bizet, our gardener. But since my friend Maggie has not had the opportunity to learn your language, I'm sure you ladies will understand why I prefer to speak English in her presence."

"Very *gallant*, Monsieur," said Marie. "I didn't catch your name?"

"Moses," he replied. "At your service."

"Mr. Moses," said Francine. "We are ever so tired and thirsty. Perhaps you might show us a place to rest and get a drop to drink. The dust from your roads has parched my throat entirely."

"Please follow me," said Moses. "My home is humble, but everything I have is at your disposal."

Maggie couldn't believe that these arrogant mice were so charmed by the simple Moses. She watched them trail after Moses until Philippe took her forepaw.

"Shall we follow, my dear?" he asked, smiling. His wonderful brown eyes sparkled from the light of Moses' retreating candle. How could Francine and Marie have the least interest in Moses when they traveled with a mouse as fine as Philippe? She couldn't understand it.

When they were tucked into Moses' nest, Maggie expected that surely the ladies would be appalled by his limited furniture and his crude wallpaper made of newspaper clippings, but this was not the case. They sipped tea from his broken cups and listened with great interest to his stories about various escapes from enemies such as foxes and groundhogs. Francine even went so far as to compliment him on his strong muscles. Maggie thought she had endured all she could bear when in sauntered the dreaded Evangeline and Brutus, looking very proud of themselves.

"What do we have here?" asked Evangeline. "I've never seen such a dressed up pair of rodents. I used to think my sister Maggie was as vain as a mouse could get. Looks like I was wrong."

"Your sister?" asked Marie, giving Maggie a disdainful look.

"You must forgive her," Maggie said reluctantly. "She's just given birth to a nest full of babies. She's not herself." She grabbed Evangeline by the arm. "And I hear them calling for their dear mother right now," she said, trying to escort Evangeline back to the tunnel.

"Oh no, dearie," said Evangeline. She shook her arm away from Maggie. "It's not likely I'd want to miss all the fun . . . having a spot of tea with the likes of these beauties."

"Tea is it?" questioned Brutus. He gestured toward Philippe. "You look like a man who'd enjoy a spot of something with more kick to it."

Maggie was surprised when Philippe seemed pleased at the prospect of stronger spirits. In fact, she was more than surprised. She was shocked. Nothing was happening the way she had dreamed. She tried to think of what Dolley would do under similar circumstances, but her imagination failed her. Dolley would simply never get herself into such a sorry state.

"I have an idea," said Moses. "I saw the cook preparing some tea cakes just before you arrived. If my nose serves me right, they were gingerbread cakes which she always dusts with sugar. They'll be just the thing to revive you."

"Whatever you say, Moses," commented Francine with a coy smile that showed just a glimpse of her ivory teeth. "I'm sure we can trust your judgment to serve us only the best."

"Well aren't you just the sweetest little mousie," said Evangeline with a sneer. "You're so sweet, in fact, I'm afraid if I stay here another moment, I'll get a toothache. I'll lose my bloody lunch, in fact. I'd rather be home with my screaming babies than listening to the likes of you." She gave a loud sniff and waddled her way through the door. Maggie sighed with relief at a small mercy.

"And how about you?" Brutus asked of Philippe, throwing his arm around the Frenchman's shoulders. "Care to have a little nip with me?"

"I was privileged to taste some superb wine at Mr. Jefferson's home," said Philippe, "so I think . . . in the interest of oenology, the study of wine, you understand . . . I should try Mr. Madison's cellar as well."

"Excellent," said Brutus heartily. "You won't be sorry."

Maggie shook her head in disbelief as the two mice withdrew, arm in arm, looking as if they had been friends for years.

"All right, Maggie," said Moses. "You entertain the ladies, and I'll be back shortly with a freshly baked tea cake."

The room was suddenly dead quiet. Francine and Marie appeared to be as uncomfortable as Maggie. She could think of nothing to say to such pretentious mice.

Finally, Francine spoke. "Monsieur Moses appears to be a man of many abilities," she said.

"He has a family, yes?" asked Marie.

Maggie knew exactly what was on Francine's mind. "No family," she replied, thinking of how awful it would be if Moses became interested in one of these terrible mice for a wife! It was bad enough to endure them for the space of a few days, but what if they lived at Montpelier for a lifetime? The thought of such a thing made her sink to the floor and put her head on her forepaws. She had thought this day would be the best of her life. Instead it was turning into the worst.

Danger Is In The Air

CHAPTER NINE

What Next?

Dear Diary,

I must confess once more that I have been the most foolish of mice. My pride. It is my pride that has caused my downfall. I remember when I was a young mouse, taking such a great interest in designing and sewing little caps for myself. At the sight of me preening before a mirror, my mother warned that "pride cometh before a fall." How right she was. I now see myself through the eyes of our French visitors for what I really am . . . a silly country mouse pretending to be above my station in life. But I must say that if Francine and Marie are examples of what it means to be sophisticated ladies, then I want no part of it. Their dresses may be elegant, but their hearts are shabby indeed.

Surely my dear friend Moses is not deceived by their fancy ways. Yes, I say **dear**, because it has taken the arrival of the French to make me appreciate his sterling American virtues. His ability to read and to speak

French has never made him think he is better than his mouse brothers and sisters. Oh, I have much to learn.

And that Philippe!! My head was turned by his charming manners and his green velvet waistcoat. And do you know what he did? He went off with Brutus and drank himself into a stupor. We had to carry him back to his bed.

The banquet for the marquis and other guests is this afternoon. Anna will be joining me, but, sadly, so will those prissy French girls and that disappointing Philippe. I intend to model myself after Moses and be polite and unpretentious. I will. Really, I will.

* * * *

Maggie, Anna, Moses, and the three French visitors arrived early before the celebration and positioned themselves under the elaborately carved mahogany sideboard where they had an excellent view of General Lafayette as well as the Madisons. Francine had informed Maggie that Lafayette preferred to be addressed as General rather than Marquis, but he was still "the marquis" in her heart.

Earlier in the day, the marquis had presented Mrs. Madison with the gift of two handsome porcelain urns, as well as a matching bud vase. These sat on the long mahogany table in the center of the room and were filled with the last of the season's blossoms from Dolley's garden. The table sparkled with the best china, silver, and crystal, a vision to behold. The banquet guests included the general, of course, and also his son, his secretary, Mr. Jefferson's grandson, and a collection of neighboring landowners. There were many toasts to the general's years of service to America, but none more eloquent and brief than Mr. Madison's. He stood with great energy for a man of seventy-four years.

"To liberty," he said, raising his glass. "It has virtue for a guest and gratitude for a festival."

The marquis nodded his head in thanks as all at the table added, "Hear, Hear."

Maggie thought she had never seen a more magnificent gathering. Surely even the snobbish French mice had to be impressed. She noticed Marie eyeing Dolley's costume, a green dress with matching turban. Her precious pearls glowed in the candlelight as she engaged in a lively conversation with the general.

"Mrs. Madison is very taken with the turban, I see," said Marie. "How quaint."

Quaint? Maggie was sure that the description was not a compliment.

"She is quite the conversationalist," added Philippe in an offhand manner.

"I'll have you know," said Maggie, "It is a well-known fact that Mrs. Madison accomplished as much in Washington with her parties as Mr. Madison did with his politics!"

"I meant no offense," said Philippe, sputtering. "I have nothing but the respect for Mrs. Madison." He brandished the smile that Maggie had found so charming only the day before—the day before, that is, before he had chosen to drink with Brutus rather than to socialize with her.

"Oh, Auntie!" said Anna excitedly. "Thank you for inviting me here. I have never seen such beauty on a table. Will the Madisons be serving ice cream?"

Maggie appraised her niece's fresh beauty and appreciated it more than ever. She gave Anna a pat on her plump cheek. "You can be sure Mrs. Madison is serving the best of everything, my dear. And she is famous for her ice cream."

"Food, food, and more food," lamented Francine. "I have seen enough of these feasts to last a lifetime. Everywhere we travel, you people try to stuff the general as if he is a goose."

"Please, Mr. Moses," said Marie with a sweet smile on her face. Too sweet, thought Maggie. "Perhaps you can show us to the parlor where we might get some relief. I must escape this frantic menagerie."

Maggie wasn't sure of the meaning of the word *menagerie*, but the way Marie said the word, she could tell it wasn't good. Maggie was sad to leave the party in the dining room, for she knew she would never again see such an array of splendid foods and elegant company. She had seen enough, however, to provide memories for a lifetime.

As they skittered past the servants' feet, Marie did not stop talking. "You cannot believe the things we have already seen in your country. Since we arrived in New York City in the middle of August, we have been celebrated everywhere."

Francine joined Marie in telling of visits to Harvard and Yale, to dinner at the president's house, to parades and balls and constant ceremonies.

"It has been very tiring as you must imagine," Francine added dramatically.

Moses led them to the parlor, which was calm and quiet for the present.

"Ah," said Philippe upon seeing the portrait of George Washington hanging on the wall. "The great friend of our general. We have most recently visited his tomb."

"A pianoforte," exclaimed Marie. "Will there be entertainment after dinner? Do you expect a musician?"

"Moses can play the piano," piped up Anna. "I've heard him do it."

Maggie remembered the evening when she thought she had heard Moses singing a song to the piano's tune. Maybe it was not a dream.

"Oh *merveilleux*," said Francine, clapping her tiny paws together. "Do you play Mozart?"

"I've never heard of that song," Moses replied.

Francine and Marie began to laugh at the same time, the sound growing louder and louder.

"Mozart is a *composer*," said Marie, barely able to speak from laughter. "Not a song, silly boy."

Maggie was furious at their rude manners. These were supposed to be fine ladies?

"Stop it," said Maggie. "You have no right . . ."

Moses interrupted her. "I'm just a plain Virginia mouse," he said modestly. "I sing the old folk songs. And sometimes I make up my own."

"Makes up his own?" shrieked Marie. "With all the fine music there is to play?"

The two mice were so overcome with laughter that they collapsed on the ornate carpet, helpless with giggles. Philippe had the good grace to be embarrassed and avoided the two silly girls. He strolled around the room, looking at the artwork. And whereas there was far too much conversation in the dining room for anyone to notice the roaring of two discourteous mice, the sound did catch the attention of *someone* in the house. A someone who had quite an interest in the pursuit of small, delicious mice.

Maggie heard the flap of wings before she saw Polly's immense body looming above them in the air.

"Watch out," she cried to the two rollicking mice. "Run for cover," she said as she grabbed Anna's paw to pull her niece under the piano. Philippe had the presence of mind to dart under the Campeachy chair where he hovered, his eyes filled with fear. Still Francine and Marie were unaware of Polly's presence, because they were making so much noise of their own. Then Polly, in all her colorful dangerousness, swooped down upon them, lifting up Marie by the tail, taking her high into the air, before she accidentally dropped her on the piano keys. Marie landed quite firmly right on the key of middle C. She appeared dazed by her botched kidnapping, and suddenly Moses grabbed her paw and pulled her from the piano to safety under the nearest chair.

Frozen by fear, Francine remained on the carpet, sobbing, calling for help in French. "Au secours," she screamed, words that the French-speaking Polly knew very well. The macaw let out a cackle that sounded like a laugh and circled in the air preparing for another dive. She flew as if she owned the room, broad flaps of her strong wings stirring the air. It was only a matter of seconds before she returned to make an attempt to capture Francine in her powerful beak.

Maggie had left Anna's side and was making a dash for Francine. She crossed the patterned carpet and slammed into Francine's side, propelling them both under the sofa just as Polly began her descent.

"Squawk," said the bird angrily as she had to rise to avoid hitting the sofa.

Francine continued to sob as Maggie tried to calm her by stroking her trembling body.

"It's all right," said Maggie. "She'll go away now. Don't you worry."

But Polly didn't go away immediately. She perched on the mantel for all of fifteen minutes, spouting French words and watching her prey to make sure they didn't dare to move. Maggie was grateful that no one had been hurt, but she was heartsick nevertheless as she crouched beneath the sofa, listening to Francine's continued sobs. When the French mice talked about their experience in the Madisons' home during the remaining part of their trip, they wouldn't mention the charm and hospitality of the experience. It would be only Polly's attack that they remembered. But then again, because of the murderous Polly, they probably wouldn't mention their visit to Montpelier at all.

A Happy Ending

CHAPTER TEN

Farewell

Dear Diary,

The general leaves tomorrow. His visit has shown us all what a remarkable man he continues to be. He is a great soul. At the age of sixty-seven, he has proven that his love of liberty is undiminished. He has engaged in long discussions with Mr. Madison about the evils of slavery, and Mr. Madison has agreed with him in every particularity. Mr. Madison and his neighbors all have the same opinion—that a country founded on the principles of freedom cannot allow slavery to continue.

I have seen little of the French mice over the past two days. I assured them that Polly never goes into the guest bedroom, so they have chosen to remain in its safety. I bring them food, but we have nothing more to say to each other. I'm certain they are eager to leave this place, and I shan't be sorry to see them go.

Anna reminded me that I had promised the doll Josette that I would do all in my power to see that she was *tucked away in the general's luggage so that she could return to her home in France. Anna and Moses helped me carry Josette to the guest bedroom, and Francine and Marie did not object to her joining them. I think they are pleased to have someone else on the trip who speaks their language.*

I must say that this visit has allowed me to evaluate my ideas on the superiority of all things French. I am pleased to say that General Lafayette is as superb in every way as I had anticipated. I still believe that French fashions are the most exquisite of any in the world. On the subject of French mice, however, I have to say that they did not measure up to my expectations.

We have one thing left to accomplish before they leave. Philippe told me that the general is gathering soil from each state; he plans to have the soil scattered on his grave in France after he is buried. Moses and I will collect a portion of good Virginia dirt, seal it in a jar, and stow it in his luggage before he departs this afternoon. A little of my dreams will go with it.

* * * *

After the departure of Lafayette and his people, Maggie waited until it was completely dark before she lit a candle to venture out and survey the guest room. She was dressed in a simple muslin shift, her head covered with a ruffled cap. The servants had already stripped the bed of linens and replaced them with clean sheets. Maggie sniffed the air, enjoying the fresh smell of soap.

But there was one scent that was unfamiliar. She followed the aroma until she discovered a yellow ribbon under the bed, forgotten by the French guests. Even though it was unlikely anyone would come into the room at such a late hour, she wanted to examine the ribbon in her own nest, so she put it under her left arm and hurried back to her chambers.

She spread the ribbon across the floor, smoothing out the wrinkles. A shiver of joy surged through her body as she realized what a treasure she had found: on the ribbon were stamped the words, "Welcome Lafayette," as well as a reproduction of the general's handsome, noble face. The perfect keepsake of a perfect patriot.

She was draping the ribbon across the top of her finest mirror when she heard faint strains of music coming from the piano downstairs. This time she was determined to investigate the source of the music for herself. She was sure it could only be Moses at this late hour, so she slipped a robe over her gown and headed down the stairs.

When she drew closer to the parlor, she confirmed that it was Moses singing in a clear tenor voice. As soon as she could make out his words, she stopped sharply and reared back on her hind legs. She could hardly believe what she was hearing, for he was singing about none other than her, Maggie Mouse. These are the enchanted words she heard:

I love you, Maggie,
You are an answer to my dream.
I love you, Maggie,
You are more than what you seem.

I love you, Maggie,
You bring the sun into my life.
I love you, Maggie,
And I want you for my wife.
Maggie, Maggie, Maggie.

Maggie felt her eyes fill with tears. He loved her! Even though he had seen her at her most foolish. More than once! Even when he compared her to the two most elegant mice imaginable.

She entered the parlor slowly, wiping her eyes. Moses stopped playing as soon as he discovered that she had entered the room. He wore an expression of horror, as if Polly were about to attack him.

"Maggie," he began, but he couldn't seem to say more.

Maggie climbed up the piano leg and joined him on the black and white keys.

"Thank you, Moses," she said simply. "I don't deserve such a beautiful song."

"Oh, Maggie," he added. He couldn't look her in the eyes.

"You have forgiven me?" she asked, placing his paw in hers tenderly.

"Forgiven you?" he asked in astonishment. "There was nothing to forgive. You are the most beautiful . . . the bravest . . ."

"The most foolish," added Maggie.

"You are the perfect mouse for me."

They sat looking at each other with love, and Maggie made no more attempts to clarify his opinion of her. She knew love was said to be blind, and she was so grateful for this brave, strong, brilliant, blind mouse at her side.

THE END

AND GUESS WHAT?

When experts restored the Madison home, return-ing it back to the way it was during James and Dolley's day, they really did discover a mouse's nest. It was tucked into the Madisons' bedroom wall, a nest that had been hidden for over a hun-dred and eighty years.

When they looked inside the nest, they found a strip of upholstery fabric, a bit of hand-painted wallpaper, a piece of newspaper and a scrap of paper with these words in James Madison's own handwriting, "Mother would."

Now you know what Mr. Madison meant when he wrote, "Mother would." And you know who lived in that special nest: Maggie Mouse, that's who.

ACKNOWLEDGMENTS

I want to thank all of the many hardworking Montpelier staff members who gave me guidance throughout the writing of this book. These people don't just work at the Madison home; they have a great dedication to bringing the Madison family to life.

I want to recognize Peggy Vaughn who gave me inspiration and encouragement from the beginning. Thanks also to Beth Taylor who answered many questions, to Dr. Matthew Reeves who showed me pictures of the rodent runs that were discovered in Montpelier's basement and helped me to imagine the downstairs life of Moses and his friends. Thanks to Maggie Wilson who actually found this important mouse's nest and without whom there would be no story.

Thanks to Rick Payne who manages Montpelier's gift shop and who will make Maggie available to visitors, to Michael Quinn, President of Montpelier who has shepherded the restoration of Montpelier and to John Jeanes who actually supervised the work.

I thank Rangeley Wallace and Evelyn Bence for their editing help. Also thanks to E.J. Mudd, Mary Beth Busby, and Ellen Atwell. A special thanks to Paula Veshore for her whimsical and sensitive illustrations.

And most of all I thank my husband, Bill Lewis, for his dedication to Montpelier . . . and to me.

12411061R00070

Made in the USA
Charleston, SC
03 May 2012